The Songs of Lilith

The Songs of Lilith

A Tree of Poems

WRITTEN AND
ILLUSTRATED
BY A. J. SAKEN

ISBN: 0692969969
ISBN 13: 9780692969960

CONTENTS

Avarice
Medusa

Vanity
Marie Anoinette

Wrath
Artemisia

Lust
Jezebel

Pandora's Box
Lucifer

Lost Souls

John 12:25
He that loveth his life shall lose it; and
he that hateth his life in this world shall
keep it unto life eternal.

Leah

1

Cupio Dissolvi*

One lonely night,
Acedia took over my desolate,
My darkened soul.
When night was dark,
And murky shadows fused into my airy gloom,
I couldn't sleep, nor weep.
I wanted to expire.

These murky shadows, devil aides, unholy sleuths,
They triumph when your body's labored
And your mind's unsound.
And when they do, they merge with you;
Your spirit may be lost
Unless you probe and gather all the might;
Some do, some don't...
I couldn't.

Although I was once strong,
That night I wasn't.
I couldn't fight the shadows, not anymore,
And so they took me on a journey—
Or was I dreaming? Perhaps I was!
But, nonetheless, the dream was real
In this unholy lore.

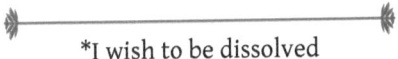

*I wish to be dissolved

II

Somnium*

I had a dream I went into the afterlife—
I met the chief commander, Lucifer,
Among the other evil gods.
The place where all the darklings dwell,
The place called Hell.

It is magnificent and vast;
And seven Kingdoms it unites,
And every Kingdom is its own Hell
Wherein the Queens are placed to oversee
The sinners, and make them pay.

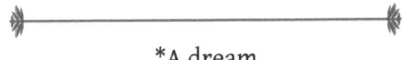

*A dream

III

Genius Loci*

Lilith
Said she, her name was Lilith,
Exquisite and divine,
Appeared she before me,
To greet and show me Kingdoms
Of hell, and be my guide.

Lilith
Said she, her name was Lilith,
Was waiting for me here
When I arrived,
Between these walls,
Among these chambers,
To lead me through the Hell
And show me afterlife.

*A spirit of place

IV

Reginae Infernum*

The Queen of Vanity is
Lovely Marie Antoinette.
The mistress of her trade,
She was so vain her body perished
Wearing the latest fashion trends.

The Queen of Envy is dear Nefertiti.
So envious she was of Gods
That she decided to become one.
The deed was foolish, so she's here.
Deservingly, she's serving under Gods.

The Queen of Greed is poor Medusa.
She's paying for the sins
Her curse compelled her to commit.
Alas, she's here to cleanse her soul
And have it back anew.

The Queen of Rage is Artemisia.
There's no one better suited for the role.
For she's a real monster,
Unmerciful,
Rage dressed as a girl.

The Queen of Lust is Jezebel,
And all her spirits —
And there are millions of them.
They fly around gathering all sinners
And properly they punish them.

At last, it's me, my dear;
Your guide through Hell.
My name is Lilith,
And I'm the ruling Queen of Hell.

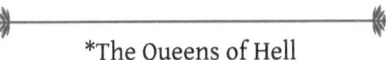

*The Queens of Hell

9

Deception

John 8:44
Ye are of your father the devil..
he is a liar, and the father of it.

Lilith

V

In Propria Persona*
(Lilith's Song)

I oversee the Kingdom of deception,
It is particularly dear to my kin.
It caters solely to those who've fallen victim
To the very first of human sins.
And now this Kingdom serves as the pioneer
That spread the roots
And gave us this entire Hell.

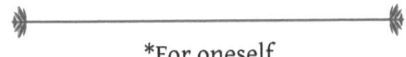

*For oneself

VI

Fons Vitae Caritas*
(Adam's Song)

The Moon is not alone,
The Sun is always near.
The river flows into her lover, the lake.
All animals are paired lovingly,
So I should have a perfect mate.

Rejoice, O Jophiel, for God has heard my prayers,
My mate now stands before me;
So beautiful, so pure.
Her name is Lilith,
The loveliest of names I ever knew.

Her name is Lilith.
I love her dearly;
The very first female to ever grace this Earth.
She's my companion, my wife, and my forever,
I now need only her and nothing more.

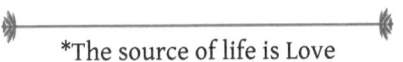

*The source of life is Love

VII

De Nobis Fabula Narratur*

And so it was...
My Adam ordered me
To lie beneath him.

And I refused,
For made of dust I am
Just like him;
And, therefore,
I am his equal.

*Their story is our story

VIII

De Profundis*
(Lilith's Song)

Obedience is not my virtue
O dear Adam, let me be
For God created us as equals;
My essence needs to roam
And I am free.

I long to see the sights beyond the horizon.
I want to know what's over the hills—
Can't be enslaved forever here.
I need to roam;
For I am free.

This garden is all we have, you argue;
It's all for us, and that's all you need,
But I want more, I know not what,
I need to find it.
I need to roam alone,
My soul's unbounded,
For I am free.

Please hear me, dear,
My sweet Adam.

A caged bird,
I'm here.
So let me go,
And let me live.

Alone.
For God created us as equals.
I need to leave,
For I am free.

IX

Fortis Et Liber*

Away from Adam,
I was getting ready for my journey.
But Adam wouldn't let me go.
I had to utter the magic name of God,
(YAHWEH)
Which freed me
And gave me strength;
It gave me wings.

Up, up and away,
And I was gone;
Away from Adam,
And away from Eden.

So free.
So liberated.
All I could feel was ecstasy.

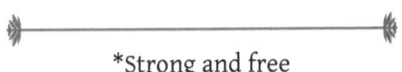

*Strong and free

X

Lucifer

Among the brightest of celestial beings
Was Lucifer, the Morning Star.
The wisest and the strongest of all God's creations,
He was the favorite of the most High.

Yet Lucifer's heart was corrupted by envy;
He started to fancy himself a God—
Wanted ascension higher than Heaven,
Wanted to act as the God most High.

XI

Divide Et Impera*
(Lucifer's Song)

Come ye, my fellows
And listen to me.
I am now telling you to join my leagues.
Against the Almighty,
I know you intrigued.

I have the free will,
So let's do the choosing.
Did He create us for his own amusing?

Come ye, my fellows,
And listen to me.
I'm now telling you to join my leagues!
No servitude will be given to Him
For we are the elite!
No longer will be protected His throne of glory
For I am as powerful;
This will be my territory!

Come ye, my fellows,
And listen to me.
Do ye your choosing immediately!
Those who will choose to dispute me
Will be thrown out of Heavenlies

Dutifully!

All of ye have the enormous powers to rule;
I will give each one of you your own domain,
Each will have his own Throne of glory,
Each will be God in his own authority.

Come ye, my fellows,
And listen to me!
I am now telling you to join my leagues!
'Tis the time to be our own creators,
For finally Heavenlies will be ours;
Those against us will be devoured.

*Divide and rule

XII

Desiderantes Meliorem Patriam*

And war broke out in Heaven.
And Lucifer, the Morning Star,
Was cast down to Earth,
His wings cut off,
And turned into a heavy spar.

His demons followed him—
The fallen angels,
They knew not
Heaven was forever out of reach
And glory was forever taken
The premier law they now have breached.

Now cast in darkness,
They wallow in deceit—
Incessantly jealous of the human race,
All they can do is deceive.
Cast out of Heaven,
Their glory is gone.
Trickery is now their main concern.

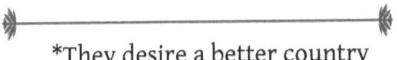

*They desire a better country

33

XIII

Samael*

I flew to the Red Sea,
And sat there on rocks,
Singing my song of pure gayness.
Looked up and saw many bright lights
Falling on Earth and all around me.

Let it be known
That the angels
Came down to Earth.
Among them was Samael.
O, how magnificent he was!

Come here, said I,
Let me know you.
Heavenly creature,
Tell me your story.

Thus, he began:
We're the angels,
The fallen.
The war is now lost,
Exiled from Heaven,
And it's our folly.

His body was shaken;
He was lost,
He was lonely,
He knew not of this Earth.
So I became his only...

XIV

Vindicta*

Adam was furious I was away.
He had three angels fetch me—
But no, I said,
No way I'm going back there,
All I need is here with me.

Yes, they persisted,
With us you must come,
Lest the Almighty will punish you!
Hundreds of your children,
Each day one will die.
If you will stay here,
This is your warning.

I had no choice but to refuse their taunt;
How could I leave my Samael beloved?
As they have promised
So they have done
A hundred of my children away,
My adored ones.

In cruel pain,
I was sobbing
Vengeance I wanted, I hissed:
Adam will pay,
My aides were nodding,
And I turned my pain into deceit.

XV

Mundus Vult Decipi, Ergo Decipiatur*

So I flew to Eden,
To have my revenge.
I knew not what or how to do it.
And then I heard him talking to Eve,
Telling her of fruits forbidden.

I schemed to lure Eve,
For she seemed vain.
For that I have turned into a serpent,
Told her she's beautiful,
She could be a God:
Just eat the fruit, the forbidden.

Worked as a charm,
My wicked plan,
She ate the fruit, the forbidden.
She had her Adam try it as well;
Both ate the fruit, the forbidden.

They opened their eyes,
Now they could see,
Naked they were all this time,
Looking for clothes,
Screaming for them.

How could we do this?
Embarrassed.

God had His fury
Directed at them.
Told them they won't be forgiven.
Lost their privilege,
Cast out of Eden,
Lost and forever misgiven.

*The world wants to be deceived, so let it be deceived

XVI

Tertia Oculus*

Old as the World,
This story goes,
Adam and Eve.
The deceived—
All their seed
That walketh this Earth
Are with their third eye closed.

*The third eye

Envy

1 Corinthians 3:3
For ye are yet carnal:
for whereas there is among you
envying, and strife, and divisions,
are ye not carnal, and walk as men?

Nefertiti

XVII

Nefertiti*

I am in Hell,
Above me is the land of Egypt;
Our Egypt,
Our Holly land.
The land that gave us love and freedom;
To us—
The children of the Nile.

*The name Nefertiti means "A beautiful woman has come"

XVIII

Locus Standi*

Come, child, and hear my story.
I ruled the land of Egypt by my husband's side;
He was the great Akhenaten, Pharaoh, and my God.

Come, child, and hear my story.
A story worth a thousand words,
A thousand years,
A thousand sorrows,
A thousand souls.

Come, child, and hear my story.
Malqata, Egypt, is where my story starts...
I was alone among five hundred consorts.
The royal harem in old days served as a palace
For breeding royalty,
And I was handpicked by Queen Ty.

Djhutmose, the Crown Prince of Egypt, died young.
The next in line was my Akhenaten.
When he became a Pharaoh,
I, Nefertiti, became a Queen—
And later, Pharaoh:
The first female Pharaoh
In my own right!

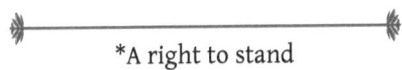

*A right to stand

XIX

Combinatio Nova*

Old Egypt had a religious system:
The cult of Amun was prevalent,
A fundamental power throughout all our land.
When I was Queen,
They worshiped Amun,
Before they fused him with the Sun God, Ra.

We, royal couple, worshiped the new holy being.
We called it Aten, the Sun God.
We built him temples greater than that of Karnak.
All out in the open,
The opposite of what the cult of Amun had.

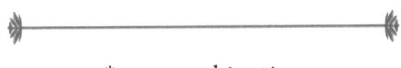

*New combination

XX

Cuius Regio, Eius Religio*

We left Thebes behind,
And moved to greet a new dawn.
We built Amarna:
Our beautiful new home.

Amarna,
The city devised to adulate the Sun.
Akhenaten and I created a new plan,
Through Egypt's new era.
With our new God, the Sun.

We tried to create a new Heaven,
To bring the new Sun to the land.
Instead, we headed for disaster:
A religious crisis became our master.

*Whose realm, his religion

XXI

Invidia*

Akhenaten had passed;
I was raised as a ruler
Before Tutankhamen grew up.
But being a Queen and Pharaoh
Still wasn't enough.

A Goddess was clearly a title
A Queen would desire, I believed.
My people hailed me as their new Goddess.
My face was adorned on their walls.

But Queen of Egypt, Goddess, Nefertiti
Envied the *real* Gods.
For still I knew I wasn't the Goddess
They furtively prayed to at night.

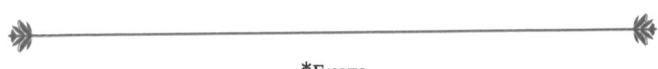

*Envy

XXII

Deo Et Patriae*

So envious was I of Gods!
That I had everyone kneel to me.
And I declared myself a God.
For that, Eternal curses marked me.

My fault was not in calling myself a God
But in not calling everyone a God,
For I am not the only God
You are a God, too.
See, we are all Gods.

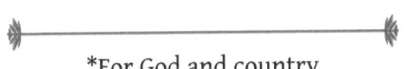

*For God and country

65

XXIII

Clavis Aurea*

So here I am, my child,
In all this sea of envy;
The second Kingdom of eternal Hell.
I rule this place as I ruled Egypt;
I choose the souls worthy to be placed in my domain.

I, Nefertiti, Queen of Egypt,
The rarest beauty of the Nile,
The perfect Queen,
The best of Queens,
Fell victim
To mere deadly sin.

And here I am;
I live forever
In the realms of worlds not seen by naked eyes.
And you, my dear, are among those chosen
To crack the code and enter this dark realm.

*Golden key

XXIV

Historia est Vitae Magistra*

Old as the World
This story goes:
Abel and Cain paint the picture.

Green with such envy,
Jealous and spiteful,
Cain found himself toward Abel.

He couldn't approve
The Lord's disapproval
Toward himself and his offer.

Envious was he
Of his own brother;
Killed him before their God's altar.

*History is life's teacher

Avarice

Proverbs 1:12-13
Let us swallow them up alive
as the grave; and whole,
as those that go down into the pit.
We shall find all precious substance,
we shall fill our houses with spoil.

Medusa

XXV

Regina Medusa*

I am the ruler of this particular domain,
As I'm the greediest of all,
It so appears.

It so appears I devoured many souls,
As any man who ever looked me in the eyes
Was smitten by my deadly beauty,
And immediately turned to stone.

The sins my soul now carries
No one ever could dispute.
The load is heavy,
But someone needs to bear it.

So here I am,
A Queen of greed in Hell.
But hear me, dear,
This fate I didn't choose.
My soul was tricked.
It was a curse I had to carry.

My golden locks were gone,
Replaced by snakes,
My baby blues with slits,
My girly innocence with deadly beauty.
They were a curse—
Athena's play.

*Queen Medusa

XXVI

Poseidon

I was a priestess of Athena in my human day,
Though I was never quite a human.
I was a daughter of the Earth and Sea,
But mortal unlike Gods,
I chose the life of celibacy.

I was a priestess of Athena till one day
I had to fetch some water from the sea,
For rituals they said;
And so I went without knowing,
That I'd come back a different person,
And even more—
A woman.

For on my mission I met a man,
A man so prominent in figure,
Such beauty I have never seen,
A man made fleshly out of water.

He was the ruler of the sea, Poseidon.
My heart stopped beating when I saw him.
I had to pose to get my wits about me,
So I could talk to him when he approached me.

That morning I discovered
Things are not what they appear to be,
Sometimes not even felt until they're brazen.

I always thought that I was happy
As anyone could be,
Though when I saw him
I knew I had a void inside.
I thought that maybe I could love him.

XXVII

Cor Ad Cor Loquitur*: (Poseidon's Song)

Come, my fair maiden,
Sweet as morning dew,
Let me hold thy hands
Warm as afternoon.

Let me sing my song
For thy earnest ears,
For I know in thy heart
I could be thy dear.

Golden locks remind me
Of the sunny hues
I do so admire
Every afternoon.

I'm the God, Poseidon,
Sea is where I sleep,
Although I'll leave the waters
Just to be with thee.

Come, my dear maiden,
Let me hold thy hands;

Let me sing my song
For thy earnest ears.

Come, my fair maiden,
Leave thy cares behind,
For thou art now in the presence
Of a perfect mind.

XXVIII

Hinc Illae Lacrimae*

He was so pleasant,
This charming man,
I felt as though I needed
To be in his hands.

Ritual water I carried, I lost
Just like my senses,
My mind, and my clothes.

Now what followed,
You probably know.
Athena was filled with such envy:
Jealous of me, of Poseidon, our love.
She turned my hair into hideous snakes,
I lost my love and my beauty in heartaches.

*That is what those tears were for

XXIX

Circulus Vitiosus*

Old as the World
This story goes.
Greed has us all on our knees.

Coveting wealth,
Voracious activities,
Demands of attention—
All due to greediness.

Hear the truth, dear,
For it is clear:
Possessions won't make
Thy soul rich.

*A vicious cycle

Vanity

Psalm 119:37
Turn away mine eyes from
beholding vanity;
and quicken thou me in thy way.

Marie Antoinette

XXX

Vanitas Vanitatum*

Step in, my dear,
To my Kingdom:
Vanity grandiose!

Marie Antoinette before you,
The pleasure's mine,
The wonder's yours.

I have to say I am a Queen in Hell,
A better place I wouldn't know;
I have champagne and music,
Dancing, and an array of men.
Oh, dear,
This place is everything I need,
I've come to know.

*Vanity of vanities

XXXI

Omnia Vanitas*

Mirror, mirror, on the wall,
Who's the fairest of them all?
I would ask you, but I know.
It is I; you and I know.

Mirror, mirror, on the wall,
Who's the smartest of them all?
I would ask you, but I know.
It's not me; and we both know.

All I cared for was how I looked,
The latest fashion:
Dresses, shoes.
Deep inside I wished I could
Offer something more than looks.

Although I wasn't always vain,
I read books on how to reign.
Yes, my dream was to become a composer,
Just like Wolfgang, my friend Mozart.

But my fate addressed my future:
I had to wed a Prince, a French creature,
Whom I didn't even know,
Who despised me from the get-go.

Dreams were shattered.
Hopes were gone.
A young Princess imprisoned,
Played like a pawn.

So to fight depressive states,
I concentrated on myself:
Better wigs, curated fashion,
And champagne;
As my husband didn't give me any passion.

XXXII

Rara Avis*

One lovely afternoon at court,
I witnessed something so magnificent!
A balloon filled with air,
Flying up into the sky,
With animals on board.

Joseph and Jacques Montgolfier
Designed such beauty, such cleverness.
To think that one day a human
Could be aboard and fly away,
I almost burst my bustier.

I longed to be the little chicken
That was on board.
For though constrained in a tiny basket,
It was free;
Free of all these people
Who surrounded me.
Free, if only for a moment,
Higher than the trees.

I longed to be that little chicken.
Though not as graceful as other birds,
It had an innocence
That made it blind to hurt.

Though not as clever as other birds,
It never had to lie
Though not as beautiful as people,
It never had to pose.
And freer than I'd ever be,
And maybe, even happy, which I never was.

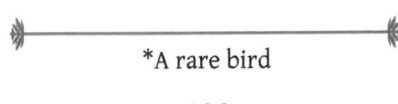
*A rare bird

XXXIII

Pulchritudo*

And vanity, my dear,
Is the most slippery of slopes.
For once you are infected,
It only can get worse.
And you will always see,
That someone else is better,
And that will be your curse

So leave vanity to those
Who care not for internal beauty,
Because the price they'll pay is high.
For outer beauty is ephemeral,
What captures heart is soul immortal;
But care none for soul
These mortals.

*Beauty

XXXIV

Saecula Saeculorum*

Old as the World,
This story goes,
Vanity wins over conscience.
Your ego is stuffed,
Such a bad luck,
For player are you,
And you're losing.

Wrath

Exodus 15:3
The Lord is a man of war, the Lord is
his name.

Artemisia

XXXV

Ira Furor Brevis Est*

To me is assigned a mighty Kingdom,
Whose name is Wrath.
For Lucifer considered me the maddest woman:
The navy captain,
Female commander,
The only lady on the ship.
The furious, the decadent, the strongest soldier they
worship.

Wrath!
This Kingdom is for those who can't contain their anger.
Wrath!
So easy it is for us to spot
It doesn't matter whose side you're on:
The good or bad, corrupted or attacked.
They all come down here,
No matter how many starts they've had.
From mere soldier to lieutenant,
All of them I've got!

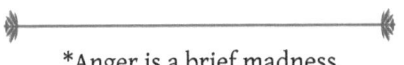

*Anger is a brief madness

XXXVI

Gaudium Certaminis*

I was in love with war and the navy,
But they were not my only love,
For then I was just a human.
I fell in love with Xerxes—
The man who made me who I was.

Great King Xerxes, King of Persia,
But to me, the King of the whole world.
I bowed my head before him,
For he was both the King and God.

And he persuaded me to fight
The battle of Salamis,
A battle I would win, no doubt.
And so I found myself in the Aegean—
I had to show him my allegiance,
My dedication and my duty.
But in my heart I wished I were
A woman that he needed.

Yet Xerxes was in love with Esther,
A Jewish girl who couldn't even hold a sword.
She wouldn't need one, though.
For only looking at her would melt a man.
She waged with looks,

Unlike me,
A demon with a sword.

Their destiny was written in the stars.
For if he hadn't loved her,
The stars would not have given Jews the Purim
Through Esther, Jewish star.

When Xerxes married Esther,
I simply could no longer be
I leaped off the cliffs of Leucas
And let my soul break free,
For I was made to rule
And be the Queen of rage in Hell for thee.

And I make sure my subjects' hearts are dark,
Their hatred fast and overflowing,
Their only wish, to kill—
They have no other worries.

And here now that's all I have:
Vengeance, hate, and lastly wrath!

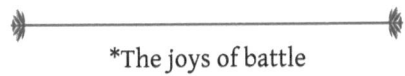

*The joys of battle

XXXVII

Fortiter Et Fideliter*

They said the oracle's words would be a warning;
They said that Greece would fall.
And Greece's fall was all I needed:
I charged my sword, said a prayer, and began my storm.

With fury I charged into the waters of the Aegean
With passion I commanded my troops.
With anger I slaughtered a thousand Grecian soldiers.
With my two hands I racked Athenian souls.

---

*Boldly and faithfully

XXXVIII

Stipendium Peccati Mors Est*

A great many warriors and soldiers
Occupy these walls:
Marcus Cassius Scaeva, Melankomas of Caria,
Aristodemus, and Roman gladiator Flamma
Are among my wounded souls.

Achilles laid his life to be remembered
Throughout the centuries.
And though his wish came through,
The price he paid was heavy,
Because his soul is bound here, too.

*The reward of sin is death

XXXIX

Infinitus Est Numerus Stultorum*

Old as the World this story goes:
Wrath shackled humans in rage.
Terror and wars are now humans' worth—
Hideous waste of lives birthed.

*Infinite is the number of fools

Lust

Matthew 5:28
But I say unto you,
That whosoever looketh on a woman
to lust after her hath committed
adultery with her already
in his heart.

Jezebel

XL

Felix Culpa*

Come in, my dear.
This is the Kingdom of Lust in Hell,
And I'm the Queen.
My name is Jezebel.

My fate brought me here,
My soul was filled with thirst.
My earthly body couldn't function,
Without satisfying earthly passions.

So here I am and rightly geared,
I know what to look for
When fallen souls go through.
I snatched mine quickly;
There's nothing new.

The poison of the mortal plane
Is pungent when they fall,
Especially the lust!
I smell and feel it;
It's their soul's tattoo.

I had my share of defeat when I was human.
But Lucifer prevailed and placed me here,
Among my kin,
As Queen.
Oh, dear!
You've got to love him,
He's the perfect King.

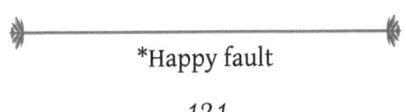

*Happy fault

XLI

Dulcius Ex Asperis*

Legend has it
Those whose bodies are not properly buried
Will roam the Earth in agony,
Without rest in prairies.
The soul will be locked in-between the realms,
Unable to move, forgotten, disarmed.

And I'm the one who knows it best:
As a prophet cried, the dogs shall eat my flesh.
The fate all folks find dreadful;
The fate they fear more than death.

Alas, I met my death, unkind as it was,
Thrown out the window, eaten by dogs.
But yet the last laugh is still mine,
Since here I am,
One of the Queens of Hell,
I hope you are charmed.

Elijah, foolish prophet, cursed me,
Defiled my character, insulted me.
Throughout the centuries, his echo traveled:
Jezebel, the whore, devourer.

And, yes, I had my sins,
I carry them proudly.
I used my gifts to order crowds.

I used my gifts to calm my King,
To move his feelings,
To make his head spin.

My reputation does precede me,
Thanks to Elijah, who lusted over me.
His odd concern with me resolved in death:
His death, mine later, the fall of Jezreel,
The Omri Empire and Israel's last breath.

XLII

Hostis Humani Generis*

Eternal enemy to human souls,
Lust is the fire of this realm.
As I'm the Queen of this domain,
Lust is the King of the human frame.

Of all desires ever known,
Lust is the Emperor of all,
For very few human beings
Can beat this basic human craving.

And if you think,
You are guilty of this sin..
I have a place for your soul here.
Rest in hell, among your kin.

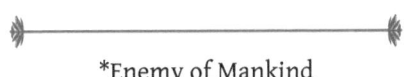

*Enemy of Mankind

137

XLIII

Infra Dignitatem*

Old as the World,
This story goes:
The spirit of Jezebel thrives.

Now more than ever,
Wanton behavior praised,
Immorality lives.

Pandora's Box

Genesis 3:5
For God doth know that in the day
ye eat thereof,
then your eyes shall be opened,
and ye shall be as gods,
knowing good and evil.

Lucifer

XLIV

In Utrumque Paratus*

At last I'm on my way to meet the Devil.
His Honor is to see me at the base of Hell.
I'm not afraid; I'm giddy even;
My time has come to meet my fate.

So many nights I've asked God for mercy,
To spare my soul the daily folly,
To let me go beyond the earthly,
To let my soul be free.

I've waited years for this encounter.
I craved to meet the holy God.
And though I'm meeting his opponent,
My heart is ready for either one.

My soul needs answers, closure, elevation.
Perhaps descent, since I'm in Hell;
And now I know it is much better
To be down here
And skip the earthly plane.

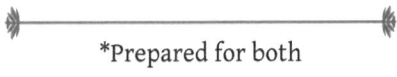

*Prepared for both

XLV

In Omnia Paratus*

Come in, my child, he said to me—
I heard his voice, but couldn't see him.
I smelled his scent, but wasn't sure.
The rush I felt had my head whirling.

The room was dark.
Where are you, spirit?
What should I say?
What names to call you?

So many thoughts ran through my mind,
Confusion had me speechless.
At last I felt his breath behind;
I closed my eyes in deep surrender.

*Ready for anything

XLVI

In Nomine Diaboli*

Open your eyes, you silly girl!
Your senses are confused.
I am not here.
The box you see upon the shelf,
That's where I am.
That's how you'll see me.

The box? I thought.
How could that be?
Pandora's box, the voice replied.
You need to open it to see.
Surprise, surprise!
Now come to me!

*In the Name of the Devil

XLVII

Speculum*

I picked up the box,
And it was heavy.
I opened it:
Nothing inside.
Look closely, I heard the Devil say,
The mirror is on its side.

The mirror? And what of all evils? I asked.
Are they not contained in the box?
They left when the box was first opened, He said.
Surely you know there weren't any locks.

Now look in the mirror and tell me—
Who does the Devil look like to you?
For what kind of being have you waited?
Do I look familiar to you?

I looked in the mirror and saw *myself.*
I can't see you, Your Majesty, I cried.
Look closely, said He.
You'll see me.
Look closely.
Don't rush.
Eternity's ours.

*Mirror

XLVIII

Imago Dei*

And now I am here with the Devil.
I traveled through Hell to be here.
The only way now I could see him
   Is through this mirror so clear.

I look and I look, but can't see him.
   The only reflection is *me*.
Your Majesty, Devil, I begged him.
   There is no one here to see.

You're wrong, little girl, said the Devil.
   There is someone there,
   And it's you.
For I don't exist; I'm your fiction.
   The Devil, my dear, is you.

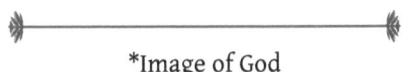

*Image of God

About the Author

A. J. Saken is a writer and editor based in New York City. She has contributed to several blogs and magazines, and is an avid student of metaphysics, mythology, and occult studies.